Raspberries!

To my children, Ted and Laura, who listened me into being a storyteller.
—J.O'C.

To the Girls in the barn.
—W.M.

Raspberries!

JAY O'CALLAHAN • WILL MOSES

PHILOMEL BOOKS • PENGUIN YOUNG READERS GROUP

WALDEN MEDIA

"Everything I touch falls flat," Simon, the egg man, mumbled as his wagon rolled into the dusty town. He could hear kids snickering, "Where'd he get that hat?"

Simon pulled his hat so far down you couldn't see his eyebrows, and you couldn't see if he was smiling, but you knew he wasn't.

No one knew that not long ago Simon had been a baker in Springfield town and was almost famous. He didn't wear the hat then. His hair was red and blazing, and his eyebrows were bushy as fox tails.

Saturday nights, whole families stood outside Simon's bakeshop, watching him and his two baker friends play basketball with the dough, and his bread rose higher than anyone's, so people came from miles around to get it.

JAM
OLD MOSES
WHEAT FLOUR
WHEAT FLOUR
SUGAR

BAKERY
FREE KITTENS
MAY
FRESH BREAD

His favorite customer was a little girl named Sally whose dress had hundreds of bright patches because her family was so poor. Every day Simon gave Sally two loaves of bread for a penny and Sally'd say, "That's not what they cost," and Simon'd say with a wink, "Surrrrrrrrrrre it is."

But when Simon's two baker friends stole all his money and ran away, he sold the shop because the joy went out of baking. After that, everything he touched fell flat, so he bought a farm a hundred miles away and started selling eggs in a little town where nothing ever happened.

PROUD ROOSTER
PROUD

One day after selling eggs in town,
Simon was clattering home when suddenly
he saw a thousand butterflies bursting out of the
woods. Then he realized it was a young woman in a dress of
hundreds of bright patches.

"Simon, I'm Sally. Remember you used to give me two loaves for a penny?"

"That's what they cost," Simon said.

"Noooooo they didn't," she said with a wink. "You helped me and my family for years. Now I have something for you." She gave him a pouch. "These are dried raspberries. Plant them today and just wait till you taste them." She waved her hand and was gone.

That afternoon, black clouds raced overhead and the wind screamed. Simon shooed the chickens into the barn and ran for his house when he remembered the pouch. He shook out the dried raspberries and the wind blew them all over his land. "Well, if they don't grow, at least I got a pouch," Simon said.

Then lightning cracked the sky and struck the barn, which leapt into flames. All the chickens were lost. "No more eggs, no way to make a living," Simon said, and jammed his hat down further on his head.

In the morning Simon opened the door and stared and stared. Everywhere he looked, he saw bushes covered with raspberries.

It was a rolling red sea with crests and waves of raspberries! He pushed his hat up just a bit and tasted one. It was so sweet he sprang in the air and sang out,

"Rasssssssperrrrrrrieeeeeees!"

He tasted another and found himself in the air again, yelling,

"Rasssssssperrrrrrrieeeeeees!"

so loud the bees stopped buzzing and the frogs watched bug-eyed. He picked more and more raspberries, singing,

"I'm gonna make a few pennies today, today.
I'm gonna make a few pennies today, hooray."

Simon headed into town with the raspberries in the wagon. The grocer, Persnickety Mr. Perkins, looked at the raspberries and snapped, "You're my egg man, not my fruit man."

Lucy Wooly, the town bully and the mayor's wife, said, "I wouldn't even buy eggs from *you*."

The barber said, “See these scissors, Simon? I cut hair, I don’t buy fruit.”
Everyone said no to Simon’s raspberries.

As Simon was leaving town that night, with the raspberries still in the wagon, Baker Willums came out of his bakeshop, barking like a sea lion, "What have you got there, Simon?"

"Special raspberries."

"Special?" he boomed. "I'll try one box. Come on in and watch a baker work."

LIVERY
FRESH
FOR SALE
RASPBERRIES

The old baker patted out the dough, poured on the berries, crimped up the tarts and put them in the oven. Simon pushed his hat up just a little bit to watch. "Help me knead my dough while the tarts are baking," the baker said.

Simon's hands dove down in the dough. He kneaded with such rhythm, Baker Willums stared, amazed.

After a while the old baker said, "My nose says those tarts are done, and they don't smell special to me! But I'll try one."

SHAMROCK
FLOUR Co.

He bit into a tart and a great wind blew the baker and he rose to his toes, shouting,

"Rassssssspberrrrrrrrieeeeeees!"

Astonished, Baker Willums roared, "Bring 'em all in! You're gonna help me bake all night."

Simon himself snitched a tart, then jumped into the air, singing,

"Rassssssspberrrrrrrieeeeees!"

The freckles almost flew off his face.

They baked bread and pies and eighty-four tarts, and in the morning Baker Willums said, "That was the best baking night of my life, but I'm tired out and I'm going to sleep, so you do the selling, Simon."

At eight o'clock sharp, Mrs. Sharp marched in. Her chin was sharp, her nose was sharp and her umbrella was sharp. "What are those odd things?" she snapped.

"Raspberry tarts," Simon said.

"Grandmother never had bumps on her tarts," she said. "I'll try one nevertheless."

Mrs. Sharp took a bite, her head shot up and she cried, "Rassssssspberrrrr

A few minutes later, Mrs. Sharp's friend, Jenny Longlegs, came in. Jenny took a bite of the tart and her hat flew into the air as she sang,

"Rassssssspberrrrrrrieeeeees!"

eeees!”

“Simon,” they both said, “how many tarts have you got?”

“Eighty-four,” Simon said.

Mrs. Sharp said, “We’ll take forty each. That leaves almost none for Lucy Wooly. She’ll be sorry she didn’t invite us to her tea.”

At noon Baker Willums beamed. “You sold almost every tart. Simon, you’re not as shy as you look.”

Just then the door flew open and the mayor’s wife, Lucy Wooly, the town bully, stormed in. “Today is my annual tea and I hear you have a wonderful tart. Did you save eighty for me?”

“Only four,” Simon said.

“You saved only four?” she shouted. “Wrap them all, Baker Willums. It’s the last time I’ll be in your shop.” She left. Baker Willums sagged.

Simon pulled his hat lower. “Everything I touch falls flat.”

That afternoon, the great tea was held on Lucy Wooly's lawn a mile out of town. Lucy Wooly looked like a mound of floating vanilla ice cream. Old Mrs. Oddbones, bent as a hairpin, shuffled to the goody table. The tarts had been cut in pieces. "Mmmmm, tarts . . ." She took a bite and flew into the air, singing,

"Rassssssspberrrrrrrrieeeeeees!"

All the ladies rushed to get a piece till it looked more like a square dance than a tea.

"Where'd those tarts come from?" someone shouted.

"Baker Willums, of course!" Old Mrs. Oddbones cried as she ran and jumped over the hedge, leapt into her carriage and shouted, "Giddyaaaap!" All the ladies followed and Lucy Wooly was left alone in the dust.

In town, people thought they heard growing thunder, then out of the billowing dust roared Old Mrs. Oddbones. “Haaayyyaaaaaah!”

“Quick, Baker Willums, a dozen raspberry tarts,” Old Mrs. Oddbones demanded. Now all the ladies were clamoring. “I’ll take a dozen.” “I want two.” It was bedlam.

“I got no tarts,” Baker Willums boomed.

“Have them at eight tomorrow morning,” Old Mrs. Oddbones said. “It’s Big Day, the birthday of the town. If you don’t, we won’t trade here anymore.” And they all left.

Baker Willums slumped. “Simon, I can’t make all those tarts by morning. It’s the end of my business.”

“No,” Simon said, pushing his hat up. “It’ll all be done—and by morning.”

Simon rushed back home, picked till his wagon was heaped with raspberries and carted them back to Baker Willums’s shop.

All night he patted out the dough, poured on the berries, crimped up the tarts and baked and baked until there were tarts all over the place.

At four in the morning Simon went out to stretch and could've sworn he heard a star call softly to him, "Rasssssspberrrrrrrrieeeeeeees!"

At eight the next morning, the band marched and played as the ladies, led by Old Mrs. Oddbones, stormed the bakeshop. Simon was selling tarts so fast his hands were flying.

Then the ladies roared into the street, handing out tarts, flinging tarts, pitching tarts to people who hadn't caught anything in years—to grandfathers, grandmothers, uncles, aunts, fathers and mothers, sisters and brothers and little babies too.

The whole town began to leap into the air around the band, shouting, "Raaaassspberrrrrrieeeeeeees!"

It looked like a street full of grasshoppers.

TOWN HALL

The band kept playing and people kept dancing, jumping, leaping, hopping, twirling, somersaulting and eating more tarts. Old Mrs. Oddbones grabbed the grocer, Persnickety Mr. Perkins, and said, "Dance with me, you old fuddy." She spun him around and Mrs. Sharp spun him right back.

Finally the mayor asked for quiet. “Usually on Big Day,” he said, “the band plays, I say a few words, and we all go home alone to our houses. But today we’re all bursting. It feels like a *real* birthday. We’re a town again and it’s all because of Baker Willums and his tarts.”

Baker Willums was just going into the bakeshop. He said, “I didn’t bake last night, Mayor. Simon did. Underneath that hat, he’s a fine man.”

TOWN HALL

Baker Willums pushed Simon out the door and the band struck up. Old Mrs. Oddbones took Simon's elbow and jittered up and down as a three-year-old girl danced around him. Just then Lucy Wooly, the town bully, bit into a tart and bounced so high Simon burst out laughing.

Everyone watched as Baker Willums reached for Simon's ugly old hat and tore it off. Simon's brilliant red hair shot up like firecrackers, and his eyebrows sparked.

As they cheered, Simon thought he saw a thousand butterflies far down the street, and he realized it was Sally waving. She knew all was well because his hat was gone and Simon's hair was red as raspberries.

When all quieted down, Baker Willums said, "This redhead here is going to join my bakeshop."

And he did.

Now when Simon comes to town, the children rush to greet him, shouting,

"Rassssssperrrrrrrieeeeeees!"

And sometimes the grown-ups do too.

Thanks to Carol Burnes, who used her poet's eye editing my story. —J.O'C.

PATRICIA LEE GAUCH, EDITOR

PHILOMEL BOOKS
A division of Penguin Young Readers Group. Published by The Penguin Group.
Penguin Group (USA) Inc., 375 Hudson Street, New York, NY 10014, U.S.A.
Penguin Group (Canada), 90 Eglinton Avenue East, Suite 700, Toronto, Ontario M4P 2Y3, Canada (a division of Pearson Penguin Canada Inc.).
Penguin Books Ltd, 80 Strand, London WC2R 0RL, England.
Penguin Ireland, 25 St. Stephen's Green, Dublin 2, Ireland (a division of Penguin Books Ltd).
Penguin Group (Australia), 250 Camberwell Road, Camberwell, Victoria 3124, Australia (a division of Pearson Australia Group Pty Ltd).
Penguin Books India Pvt Ltd, 11 Community Centre, Panchsheel Park, New Delhi - 110 017, India.
Penguin Group (NZ), 67 Apollo Drive, Rosedale, North Shore 0632, New Zealand (a division of Pearson New Zealand Ltd.)
Penguin Books (South Africa) (Pty) Ltd, 24 Sturdee Avenue, Rosebank, Johannesburg 2196, South Africa.
Penguin Books Ltd, Registered Offices: 80 Strand, London WC2R 0RL, England.

This book is published in partnership with Walden Media, LLC. Walden Media and the Walden Media skipping stone logo are trademarks and registered trademarks of Walden Media, 17 New England Executive Park, Building 17, Suite 305, Burlington, MA 01803.

Published simultaneously in Canada. Manufactured in China by South China Printing Co. Ltd.
Design by Semadar Megged. Text set in 14-point Golden Cockerel ITC. The art was done in oil on Fabriano paper.
Library of Congress Cataloging-in-Publication Data
O'Callahan, Jay. Raspberries! / Jay O'Callahan ; illustrated by Will Moses. p. cm. Summary: Once a famous baker but now down on his luck, Simon makes a living selling eggs until he is given some very special dried raspberries. [1. Raspberries—Fiction. 2. Bakers—Fiction. 3. Neighborliness—Fiction.] I. Moses, Will, ill. II. Title. PZ7.O164Ras 2009 [E]—dc22 2008048085
ISBN 978-0-399-25181-8
1 3 5 7 9 10 8 6 4 2